THE TIME MACHINE

H. G. WELLS

www.realreads.co.uk

Retold by Eric Brown
Illustrated by Felix Bennett

Published by Real Reads Ltd
Stroud, Gloucestershire, UK
www.realreads.co.uk

First published in 2008
Reprinted 2010, 2011

ISBN 978-1-906230-13-5

Printed in China by Wai Man Book Binding (China) Ltd
Designed by Lucy Guenot
Typeset by Bookcraft Ltd, Stroud, Gloucestershire

CONTENTS

THE CHARACTERS

The time traveller

The time traveller has built a time machine. Can he really travel into the future to learn what becomes of humankind?

Filby

An old friend of the time traveller, but will he believe the incredible story of strange worlds?

The psychologist

The psychologist enjoys his talks with his time traveller friend. Has the inventor gone completely mad this time?

The medical man

He thinks the time traveller's
tale is poppycock, but what does
he make of the white flowers
brought back from the far future?

The very young man

The young man really wants to believe in
time travel, yet this story of danger and death
in the future seems just too far-fetched.

Weena

Weena falls in love with the
strange man from the past.
How can she warn him of
the dangers he faces?

The Morlocks

The Morlocks live brutish lives far
underground. What is it that they
eat when they come out at night?

THE TIME MACHINE

The time traveller was explaining a very complicated matter to his friends. They sat before the blazing fire, drinking wine and listening to his words.

'You must follow me carefully,' said the time traveller. 'I shall have to explain one or two ideas that everyone takes for granted.'

'That's rather a grand claim to start with!' said Filby, an argumentative man with red hair.

'I do not mean to ask you to accept anything without reasonable ground for it,' the time traveller said.

'Then continue,' said the psychologist.

'Clearly,' said the time traveller, 'any object exists in four dimensions. It must have length, breadth, thickness – and duration.'

'Yes, I understand,' said the very young man.

'The fourth dimension of duration,' continued the time traveller, 'is just another way of looking at time. Now, some philosophical people have been asking why we cannot move in time as we move in the other three dimensions.'

'But,' said the medical man, 'you cannot move at all in time! You cannot get away from the present moment.'

The time traveller smiled. 'My dear sir, that is just where you are wrong. This is the germ of my great discovery – that it is indeed possible to move along the time dimension.'

'Surely that is against reason,' said Filby.

The time traveller smiled. 'Long ago,' he said, 'I had the vague inkling of a machine which could ... '

' ... travel through time?!' exclaimed the very young man.

'Yes, and I have experimental verification.'

Filby laughed.

'It would be useful for the historian,' the psychologist said. 'He might travel back in time to the Battle of Hastings!'

'One might visit ancient Greece,' said the very young man, 'and then there is always the future!'

The editor leaned forward. 'You said you had experimental verification,' he challenged the time traveller. 'Then let's see it. Though it's all humbug, of course.'

The time traveller smiled at his friends, then stood and left the room.

'I wonder what he's got?' the psychologist said.

'Some magic trick or other,' said the medical man.

The time traveller returned.

He was carrying a glittering metallic framework, a little larger than a small clock. He placed the mechanism upon a table, then drew up a chair and sat down.

'This little affair,' said the time traveller, 'is only a model. It is the prototype for a bigger machine.'

His friends stared at the machine.

'Now this little lever,' explained the time traveller, indicating a rod of ivory, 'sends the machine gliding into the future, and this one

sends it back in time. I am going to move this lever, and off the machine will go. It will pass into future time, and disappear.'

The editor opened his mouth to speak, but changed his mind.

The time traveller moved his hand towards the lever, then suddenly turned to the psychologist. 'No. Lend me your hand.' He took the man's hand and pressed the lever forward.

Everyone saw the lever move. There was a breath of wind, and one of the candles on the mantelpiece was blown out. The little machine on the table swung around, became faint ... and vanished!

The psychologist looked under the table. The time traveller laughed.

'Look here,' said the medical man, 'do you seriously believe that the machine has travelled in time?'

'Certainly,' replied the time traveller, filling his pipe. 'I have a much bigger machine nearly finished in my laboratory. And soon I intend to travel upon it.' He looked around at his friends. 'Would you care to see the time machine itself?'

Without waiting for a reply, he took up the lamp and led the way down a corridor to his laboratory. Here the friends beheld a larger version of the mechanism they had seen vanish, constructed of nickel and ivory and what looked like crystal.

'Are you serious?' asked the editor. 'Or is this some trick?'

'On this machine,' declared the time traveller, 'I intend to explore time. I was never more serious in my life.'

A week later the group of friends met at the time traveller's house. There was no sign of the time traveller himself, but the medical man stood before the fire with a note in his hand.

'Our friend is detained,' he told them, waving the note. 'He says we should start dinner at seven if he's not back. Says he'll explain when he arrives.'

The friends sat down around the table, and a servant brought the meal. They were about to begin when, a second later, the door from the time traveller's laboratory burst open and he staggered into the room. His coat was dusty and dirty, and smeared with green down the sleeves. His hair was disordered, and his face deathly pale.

'Good heavens!' cried the medical man.

The time traveller said nothing, but slumped into a chair and gestured towards a glass. The editor poured him a good measure of champagne. The time traveller drank it greedily, then fell to eating the plate of dinner before him.

At last he pushed the plate away. 'I was starving,' he sighed. 'I've had the most amazing adventure …'

'The time machine?' someone asked.

The time traveller smiled. 'It's true, every word of it.' Thus began his incredible story.

I told you about the time machine last week (said the time traveller) and just this morning I began my journey. I entered my laboratory and seated myself upon the time machine. I took the starting lever in one hand and the stopping lever in the other, and pressed the first.

I felt a sensation of falling, and glanced across the room at the clock. A moment before, it had said a minute past ten. Now it was nearly half past three!

I drew a breath, then pushed the starting lever to its extreme position – and night came like the turning out of a lamp, and in another moment came tomorrow.

I looked through the window and saw the sun hopping through the sky in a minute, and then a minute of darkness that was the night. The quick succession of light and darkness was painful to the eye, as night followed day in a flicker. I looked through the window. The land was misty, but the whole surface of the earth

was changed, the land melting and flowing as I
flung myself into futurity!

Soon I beheld great architecture rising
around me, more massive than any buildings
of our own time. I thought about stopping and
investigating. The dials on my machine stated
that I had travelled more than eight hundred
thousand years into the future.

Like an impatient fool, I pulled on the stopping lever too hard, and the machine shuddered and flung me through the air. I sat up and looked around me. I was in a small garden, surrounded by bushes with great purple blossoms.

I picked myself up and stared at a huge carved figure in white stone. It was a sphinx, with immense wings spread so that it seemed to hover, but was greatly worn by the weather and patched with green mould.

I thought about my amazing journey through time, and wondered what might have happened to humankind. Might they have changed into something inhuman, unsympathetic and powerful? I wondered if I might seem to them an old-world savage animal, whom they might kill.

Then I saw a group of figures wearing rich, soft robes. One figure hurried towards me. He was small, perhaps four feet high, and clad in a purple tunic, with sandals on his feet. He appeared to be a beautiful and graceful creature, but also very frail. My fear faded.

Soon I was surrounded by a group of these exquisite creatures. Their mouths were small, with thin, bright red lips, and they all had pointed chins.

They spoke to each other with sweet, soft voices, and then reached out and touched me to see if I was real. Soon their little pink hands were feeling the time machine. I quickly unscrewed the levers from the control panel and slipped them into my pocket.

One of the creatures came laughing towards me, carrying a garland of flowers, and put it around my neck. They led me past the white sphinx towards a vast edifice of grey stone, and we entered a great hall. On slabs of polished stone, raised a foot from the floor, were heaps of fruit. I recognised massive raspberries and oranges, but the other fruits were strange to me.

Perhaps two hundred of the little people were seated around the tables on cushions;

most of them were watching me as I sat down and looked upon the food.

As I ate, I attempted to tell these people about myself, but my efforts were met with surprise or laughter rather than curiosity. I asked them many questions, but they soon grew bored with my interrogations and turned away. I did learn, though, that they called themselves the Eloi.

After the meal I left the great hall and stepped into the sunlight. I met more of the Eloi, who were all alike; they wore the same clothes, and had fair hair and soft hairless faces. They followed me, laughing and chattering, and then they wandered off.

I climbed a nearby hill and viewed this far future earth from its summit. There were no small houses to be seen. Everyone, it seemed, lived in the vast buildings like the great hall. The landscape was verdant, with occasional great buildings and obelisks. I saw no hedges, and no signs of agriculture. The whole earth had become a garden.

I wondered if humankind had at last attained paradise, for it appeared that the Eloi lived off the fruit of the land. I had seen no machinery, no industry, and yet they were clothed in fabrics that had obviously been manufactured. I had seen no shops or workshops; nor had I seen anyone at work.

They spent their days playing, and bathing in the river which ran through the garden near the white sphinx.

Under these conditions of comfort and perfect security, these people had become helpless and childlike.

As I stood in the gathering darkness, I thought about my theories. Now I am almost ashamed of how simple my ideas were – and how wrong they were proved to be!

I made my way down the hill, shivering in the cooling night, and decided to find somewhere to sleep. In the light of the rising moon I saw the white sphinx, and before it the little lawn where I had arrived upon my time machine.

I looked more closely at the lawn. 'No!' I cried in despair. The time machine was gone!

Without it I was stranded here, helpless in this strange new world. I ran towards where

I had left the machine, falling and cutting my face. I told myself that someone had moved my machine, perhaps they had hidden it under the bushes.

When I came to the lawn, my worst fears were realised. Not a trace of my machine was to be seen. I ran around in circles, looking everywhere, and then looked more closely at the grass. There I saw strange, narrow footprints all around where my time machine had stood. I made out other marks in the grass, as if my machine had been dragged away up the incline towards the white sphinx, which stood upon a great bronze pedestal. There was a panel or door in its side, but with no handles or keyholes. It became clear to me that my time machine was now inside the pedestal.

I looked round to see that a small crowd of Eloi had gathered. They were watching me. I gestured my desire to open the bronze pedestal, but they turned away as if in fear. I found a stone and hammered upon the door, to no avail. Then I laughed aloud. For years and years I had toiled to get to this future age, and now I wanted nothing but to leave it!

I gave up at last and returned to the great hall. I decided that the only way to retrieve my machine was to learn more of this world and its people.

For the next few days I explored the land. From every hill that I climbed I saw an abundance of splendid buildings, and thickets of evergreens, and blossom-laden trees.

An odd feature of the landscape was the presence of several circular wells. They were rimmed with bronze, and within them I heard a thud, thud, thud, like the beating of some great engine.

That day I made a friend – of a sort. I was watching the Eloi bathing in a river when one of them was seized with cramp and carried downstream, screaming. To my amazement, none of her fellows moved to rescue her. They continued as though nothing was happening.

Hurriedly I dived into the river and saved the poor mite from drowning. I made sure she was well, then left her.

I did not expect any thanks from her – but in this I was wrong.

Later that day I was approached by the same woman, who smiled at me and

presented me with a garland of strange white flowers. I did my best to display my appreciation of the gift, and we were soon seated together in a little stone arbour, engaged in a conversation which consisted chiefly of smiles. The creature's friendliness affected me exactly as a child's might have done. Though our conversation was limited, I ascertained that her name was Weena. For the next few days she was always by my side.

Weena tried to follow me everywhere, even though she often lagged way behind, exhausted and calling plaintively. She was distressed and sometimes frantic whenever I left her, and I assumed it was childish affection that made her cling to me. At that point I did not know what fear I inflicted upon her when I left her.

Gradually I learned from Weena that fear had not yet left the world.

She was brave enough in daylight, but she dreaded the dark. Darkness to her was a terrible thing. Like all her people she spent the hours of darkness sleeping in the great halls, fearful of what lay outside.

The following day, unable to sleep, I rose at dawn and left the great hall to watch the sun rise. The moon was setting, casting a half-light upon the land. As I gazed down the hillside I could vaguely discern white figures, like ghosts. They were ape-like creatures, running quickly, and I fancied I saw a band of them carrying some dark body between them.

Curious, I ran down the hillside and paused before a bush where I had last seen one of the creatures. As I gazed, a pair of luminous eyes stared back at me from within the leaves, great red eyes beneath flaxen hair which covered its head and ran halfway down

the creature's back. I advanced and spoke. I
reached out and touched something soft. The
creature pulled away and rushed past me,
blundering through a pile of ruined masonry.

I followed, but the creature had vanished. I
came to one of the wells, and wondered if the
beast had disappeared down the shaft. I peered
down, and saw a
pair of large red
eyes looking up
at me.

As I stared,
the truth of
what I had
experienced
gradually dawned
on me. Humankind
had not remained one species, but had changed
into two distinct animals: one kind which lived
like children above ground; and the other, these
pale nocturnal beings, which dwelled in caves

far below the ground. Above ground, I reasoned, dwelled the haves, who lived easy lives of pleasure and comfort and beauty. Below ground lived the have-nots, the workers who supplied the childlike people with all their needs.

As I stared into the dark shaft, I wondered if it were these creatures – the Morlocks, I later learned they were called – who had taken my time machine. I determined to find out by penetrating their mysterious underworld realm.

At that moment Weena found me. She came skipping through the bushes, but stopped when she saw me beside the well. I climbed over the parapet. Weena stared after me and gave a most piteous cry, pulling at me with her little hands.

Determined to continue my exploration despite her protests, I climbed down, looking back only once to see her agonised face staring after me.

I clambered down the shaft for perhaps two hundred yards, by means of metal bars projecting from the rock. I was soon tired and sweating, and as I descended I heard the thudding sound of machinery grow ever louder. I looked up and saw that Weena had disappeared.

Soon I came to a small tunnel leading from the wall of the shaft, and I swung myself in there to rest. I do not know how long I lay there, but soon I was roused by a hand touching my face. Frantically, I pulled a box of matches from my pocket and struck one.

Before me I saw three stooping white creatures, who fled before the light. Cautiously I made my way along the tunnel, and the noise of the machinery grew louder. I struck another

match. I was in a vast
cavern. Great shapes
like machines rose out
of the dimness and cast
black shadows, in which
Morlocks sheltered from
the glare of my match.

Then I detected an odd smell in the air
– the stench of fresh blood – and I saw a small
table laid with what looked like a meal. The
Morlocks were carnivorous. I wondered which
animal had supplied the meat.

My match flickered and went out. Reaching
for another, I was horrified to discover that my
store of matches had run low. I had just four
left, and while I stood in the darkness, a hand
touched mine. Lank fingers came feeling over
my face, and I smelled an unpleasant odour.
I fancied I heard the breathing of a crowd of
those dreadful creatures around me. I felt hands
trying to take my box of matches. I shouted

out as loudly as I could. They backed away, but soon I felt them approaching again. They made queer laughing noises, and I confess that I was horribly frightened.

I turned and fled, unable to lose the sound of the Morlocks' footsteps as they followed me. In a moment I was clutched by several hands, trying to haul me back. I fought them off, and at last came to the end of the tunnel and the shaft. I felt for the projecting bars, and as I did so my feet were grasped from behind. But I had my hands on the climbing bars now, and

I kicked violently, disengaging myself from the creatures' clutches. Speedily, I clambered up the shaft.

At last I reached the surface and hauled myself over the edge of the shaft, staggering into the blinding sunlight. I fell upon my face. I vaguely remember Weena kissing me before I passed into unconsciousness.

When I awoke, Weena was still with me. I was now fearful of the Morlocks and the darkness of the coming night.

I planned to find some secure place to sleep, and make myself some weapon of metal or stone. I also hoped to find some means to make a fire, to frighten off the under-dwellers. Then, I thought, I would arrange some contrivance to break open the doors of bronze under the white sphinx. If I could enter those doors with a blaze of light, then I might find my time machine and escape. Weena, I decided, I would take with me back to my own time.

Carrying Weena on my shoulders, I climbed a nearby hill to get a better sense of where I was. From here I could make out a distant building, a palace of green porcelain. It was larger than the largest of the palaces or ruins I had yet seen. This difference in appearance suggested a difference in use, and I was minded to push on and explore it in the hope of finding something useful to aid my eventual return to the time machine. I was tired after the excitements of the day, and it was further to the palace than I had

at first thought. We were still some way off when darkness fell. We entered a small wood and settled for the night. Weena was soon asleep; I wrapped her in my jacket and stared up at the stars.

I no longer recognised the constellations, as so much time had passed since my own day. It came to me that everything I had known, the nations of the world, the languages, literatures, and even the memory of man had been swept out of existence. And in its place ...

I thought of what I had seen below ground, and I recalled the meat I had seen there.

My earlier theory, that the Morlocks were workers who laboured to provide the Eloi with their needs, I now felt sure was wrong. The little people, the Eloi, were mere fatted cattle, which the Morlocks preserved and preyed upon.

But the idea was too horrible! I looked at little Weena, sleeping at my side, and tried to dismiss the thought.

In the morning, after breakfasting on fruit, Weena and I reached the palace of green porcelain.

We passed through great doors into a long gallery lit by many windows. I was reminded of a museum, and indeed made out a thousand miscellaneous objects covered in thick grey dust.

In the centre of the hall was the lower part of a huge skeleton – a megatherium, I judged. Further in the gallery were the bones of a brontosaurus. I saw tall cabinets and glass cases, and the blackened remains of what had once been stuffed animals.

We moved further into the museum and came to a chamber full of vast machines, all corroded and broken down, but here I found an implement that might be of some use: an iron rod like a crow-bar.

Weena came quickly to my side, as if she had been startled. At the end of the chamber was a sloping hole in the ground, and in the dust-covered floor I made out a number of narrow footprints. I knew that the Morlocks had been here, and recently.

With Weena in one hand, and the iron bar in the other, I made my way from that chamber into a larger one. Here I saw the decaying vestiges of books, which had long since dropped to pieces.

In the next room we came upon a line of unbroken display cabinets, and in one of these I found a box of matches. Eagerly I tried them, and amazingly they still worked – the cabinet they were stored in must have been airtight.

For this box of matches to have escaped the wear of time for immemorial years was a most strange thing. Yet I also found a far unlikelier substance, and that was camphor. I found it in a small jar that had by chance been hermetically sealed. I fancied at first that it was paraffin wax, and smashed the glass accordingly, but the odour of camphor was unmistakable. I was about to throw it away when I remembered that camphor burns with a good bright flame, and makes an excellent candle. I found no explosives, however, nor any means of breaking down the bronze doors. Nevertheless, as we left the palace of green porcelain I felt greatly elated.

Night was again creeping towards us –
but I had in my possession the best defence
against the Morlocks. I had fire! I had
camphor, too, if a blaze were needed.

Carrying our finds, we entered
a small forest. We were
settling ourselves for the
night when I saw three
crouching figures in the
shadows. I lit a match –
and then I had an idea. If I
set fire to the undergrowth nearby, this would
scare the Morlocks and allow us to retreat.

I lit a pile of leaves and twigs and, carrying
a sleeping Weena, ran into the forest. For some
way I heard nothing but the crackling twigs
underfoot. After a time I made out the patter of
feet in pursuit, and the queer grunting voices
of the Morlocks.

I felt a tug at my coat, and another at my arm.

It was time to light another match. I put
Weena down and fumbled for a match. I felt soft
Morlock hands, creeping over my arms and back
– and Weena cried out.

Then the match fizzed, and I saw the
Morlocks retreat a little. I pulled the camphor
from my pocket, lit it and flung it at the
Morlocks, which drove them back into the
shadows. I picked up Weena and ran – but in
the confusion I had quite lost my way.

The Morlocks followed us, and soon I felt their hands upon me. Flinging off their clinging fingers, I felt in my pocket for the matchbox – but it had gone.

I was caught by the neck, by the hair, by the arms and pulled down. I felt teeth nipping at my neck. I rolled over, and in doing so my hand came upon the iron bar. I struggled up, and swung the bar, feeling the succulent giving of flesh and bone under my blows.

Then I saw Morlocks running – not
towards me, but as if in flight from something.
I gazed beyond them, and beheld a dull red
glow, and I understood the reason for the
Morlocks' flight. I had set the forest afire!

I looked around me for Weena, desperate
as I made out no trace of her. I blundered
about the forest, calling her name. All about
me was a chaos of fire and fleeing Morlocks.

Hours passed and at last came the white light of day, and all the while I searched for traces of Weena. At last I trudged slowly from the blackened forest, for I was exhausted as well as lame, and I felt wretched; for I was sure that, if the Morlocks had not fallen upon Weena, then the flames certainly had.

I approached the white sphinx, and came upon an unexpected thing. The bronze doors below the sphinx were open, and within the small chamber stood my time machine. I stepped inside, and heard a sound behind me.

The bronze door had slid shut – trapping me. Or so the Morlocks thought.

I heard murmuring and laughter as the creatures came towards me. I had only to fix the levers I had taken from the time machine, and then depart like a ghost.

I felt their hands upon me. Pushing them away, I clambered into the saddle of my machine.

I fumbled with the levers as the Morlocks clawed at me. At last I screwed the levers into place and pushed the first lever forward ... and then I was travelling again through the greyness of time towards safety.

At length I looked upon the dials of my machine, and understood that instead of reversing the lever, I had pushed it to go forward in time. The dial indicated that I was travelling millions of years into futurity.

Curious, I pulled on the stopping lever and brought the machine to a halt.

The sky was no longer blue, but inky black. On the horizon lay the huge ball of the sun, red and motionless.

The time machine was standing on a sloping beach, and the sea rose and fell gently. There was no sign of life, but for green moss covering nearby rocks.

Then I saw something move, a monstrous, crab-like creature as large as a table. Its evil eyes were wriggling on their stalks, and its mouth was alive with appetite; its great claws, smeared with slime, were descending upon me.

In a moment my hand was upon the lever.

I moved on a hundred years, and there was
the same red sun, the same dying sea, and
the same crustacea creeping in and out of the
weeds and the rocks. I cannot convey the sense
of desolation that hung over the world.

I pressed on into futurity, stopping ever
and again. At more than thirty million years
hence, the huge red-hot dome of the sun had
filled the heavens – and I saw that the crawling
multitude of crabs had disappeared. I looked
around me to see if any trace of animal life
remained, but I saw nothing move, in earth or
sky or sea.

And then I did see something. It was
a round thing, the size of a football, with
tentacles trailing down from it, and it seemed
black against the blood-red water.

Then, filled with despair at the ultimate
fate of our planet, I pulled on the lever and
travelled back through time to our present age.

'I know,' acknowledged the time traveller, 'that all this will seem incredible to you. But to me the incredible thing is that I am tonight back in this room, looking into your friendly faces and telling you these strange adventures.'

Filby laughed. 'What a pity you aren't a writer of stories,' he said.

'You don't believe me?' the time traveller asked.

'Well—'

'I thought not.' The time traveller turned to his friend. 'To tell you the truth, I hardly believe it myself – and yet ...'

He paused, put his hand into his pocket, and silently placed a garland of withered white flowers upon the table. 'There!' he cried. 'This was put in my pocket by Weena.'

The medical man examined the flowers. 'Odd,' he said. 'I certainly haven't seen anything like them.'

'That's because they do not yet exist,'

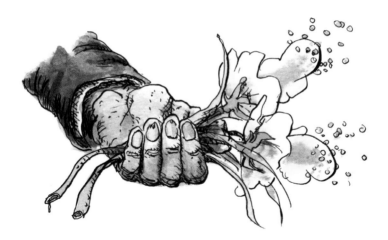

said the time traveller, taking the flowers and raising them to his nose. He looked around at his staring, silent friends.

Eventually, Filby cleared his throat. 'It's a quarter to one,' he observed. 'How shall we get home?'

'Plenty of cabs at the station,' said the psychologist eagerly.

The time traveller looked up and smiled sadly. He bade farewell to his friends, then walked alone back into his laboratory.

The time traveller vanished that day, and never returned.

Was he swept back into the past, to the stone age, or to the earlier age of the dinosaurs? Or did he go forward, into the near future, to where all the problems of our present age have been solved? Or did he travel beyond that time, to the fall of civilisation?

That was a mystery which might never be solved.

All that remained of his travels was the garland of strange withered flowers, to show that even when mind and strength were gone, gratitude and tenderness lived on in the human heart.

TAKING THINGS FURTHER

The real read

This *Real Reads* version of *The Time Machine* is a
retelling of H. G. Wells' magnificent work. If you
would like to read the full novel in all its original
splendour, many complete editions are available,
from bargain paperbacks to beautifully-bound
hardbacks. You may well find a copy in your
public library, or in your local charity shop.

Filling in the spaces

The loss of so many of Wells' original words is a
sad but necessary part of the shortening process.
We have had to make some difficult decisions,
omitting sub-plots and details, some important,
some less so, but all interesting. We may also, at
times, have taken the liberty of combining two
events into one, or of giving a character words
or actions that originally belong to another. The
points below will fill in some of the gaps, but
nothing can beat the original.

- As the time traveller begins his journey through time, his housekeeper, Mrs Watchett, enters the laboratory and walks to the garden door without seeing him. This confirms that he is no longer in the present-day world.

- Later, just before he arrives in the year 802,701, he wonders how humankind might have changed, and what advances a future civilisation might have made.

- The time traveller tells his friends about time travel in great detail. He describes the unpleasant sensation of time travelling, and his concerns about finding something solid in the space occupied by him and the machine; by travelling at speed he avoids this.

- At first he finds it difficult to communicate with the Eloi, but over time he teaches himself to speak their language. He learns that the Eloi are vegetarians, and that horses and cattle, sheep and dogs, had become extinct like the dinosaurs.

- When he first sees the white figures of the Morlocks in the twilight, he wonders if they are ghosts. He speculates on how many ghosts there must now be in the world, as thousands of years have elapsed since his own time.

- The time traveller returns to his own time, but his time machine arrives back in a different position in the laboratory to when it set out. The explanation is that in the far future it was dragged from the lawn into the white sphinx by the Morlocks. He takes his friends into the laboratory to see the time machine, which is now bent and covered in grass and moss.

- Later, one of his friends returns to his house where he finds the time traveller carrying a camera and a knapsack. The time traveller tells his friend that if he waits half an hour, he will prove that he has indeed travelled in time. His friend waits, then hears an exclamation from the laboratory. When he opens the door, the time machine has gone, but he sees a ghostly figure which vanishes as he rubs his eyes. His friend speculates what might have happened to the time traveller – to which period of history, past or future, might he have gone this time?

Back in time

H. G. Wells lived at a time of great change. Victorian Britain had a mighty empire and ruled much of the world. Many people had great wealth and prestige – but many more lived lives of poverty. H. G. Wells was a socialist who believed in equality for all people. He recognised the dangers of a divided society, and his novels and short stories are a warning of these dangers.

The Time Machine was written almost forty years after Charles Darwin published *The Origin of Species*, which introduced the important idea of natural selection. Wells played with this idea, using it to imagine that humankind might in the future develop into two distinct races.

Though earlier writers had written fantasies about magically visiting another age, *The Time*

Machine was the first novel to speculate about travelling in time using the power of science. Wells' story of time travel started a popular tradition in science fiction, and hundreds of novels and short stories followed, speculating about life in every age of the planet's history. Some consider the complex problems that might arise if you could travel back or forward in time: these problems are called paradoxes. For example, what would happen if you went back in time and met your parents before you were even born, or were able to tell stone age people about modern scientific discoveries? Would this change the future you came from?

H. G. Wells had a scientific education, and he liked to make his stories realistic. He was one of the first writers to speculate on the theory of time, and this theory is detailed in the first part of *The Time Machine*. He was also the first writer to dream about the far future, the end of life on Earth millions of years from now, and the future of the sun. At the time, many people thought that the sun would burn out in a few million years, while many scientists speculated that it would last much longer. Wells believed that the sun had been around for many millions of years and would still be burning thirty million years from now.

Finding out more

We recommend the following books, websites and films to gain a greater understanding of H. G. Wells and the world he lived in.

Books

- H. G. Wells, *Selected Short Stories*, Penguin, 1989.

- J. D. Beresford, *H. G. Wells*, Dodo Press, 2007.

- Christopher Priest, *The Space Machine*, Macmillan, 1976.

- Ann Kramer, *Victorians (Eyewitness Guides)*, Dorling Kindersley, 1998.

- Deborah Hopkinson and Nancy Harrison, *Who Was Charles Darwin?*, Grosset & Dunlap, 2005.

- Terry Deary, *Vile Victorians (Horrible Histories)*, Scholastic, 1994.

Websites

- www.hgwellsusa.50megs.com
The H. G. Wells Society official website.

- www.victorianweb.org
Interesting information about all aspects of
Victorian life, literature, history and culture.

- www.u.arizona.edu/~gmcmilla/menu.html
Fascinating website about *The Time Machine* and
H. G. Wells and his childhood, with many links.

- www.kirjasto.sci.fi/hgwells
A website all about books and writers, featuring
essays on Wells and a full list of his books.

- www.aboutdarwin.com
A website about Charles Darwin and his theory
of evolution, with information, photographs and
many links.

Films

- *The Time Machine,* directed by George Pal, 1960.
This film is faithful to most of the novel, but becomes
more of an action adventure towards the end.

- *Time After Time,* directed by Nicholas Meyer, 1979. Based on the novel by Karl Alexander, featuring Jack the Ripper who escapes justice in the time machine, and H. G. Wells himself who chases the criminal through time.

- *The Time Machine,* directed by Simon Wells, 2002. When the scientist's lover dies he attempts to change the past and bring her back to life. The future scenes contain impressive special effects, but the story strays away from the original. The director is H. G. Wells' great-grandson.

Food for thought

Here are some things to think about if you are reading *The Time Machine* alone, or ideas for discussion if you are reading it with friends.

In retelling *The Time Machine* we have tried to recreate, as accurately as possible, H. G. Wells' original plot and characters. We have also tried to imitate aspects of his style. Remember, however, that this is not the original work; thinking about the points below, therefore, can only help you begin to understand Wells' craft. To move forward from here, turn to the full-length version of *The Time Machine* and lose yourself in his science and imagination.

Starting points

- How do the time traveller's friends react to his claim that he can travel in time? How would you react to such a claim?

- How does your understanding of the Eloi change as you read the novel?

- What do you think the flowers given to the time traveller by Weena represent?

- What do you think of Wells' vision of a world without humans?

- What happens to the time traveller on his next journey? Try writing the next part of his adventure.

Themes

What do you think H. G. Wells is saying about the following themes in *The Time Machine*?

- evolution
- survival
- adventure

Style

Can you find paragraphs containing examples of the following?

- descriptions of setting and atmosphere
- the use of imagery to enhance description
- an explanation of a complicated scientific idea

Can you write a paragraph in the same style?

Symbols

Writers frequently use symbols in their work to help the reader's understanding. Consider how the symbols below match the action in this *Real Reads* version of *The Time Machine*.

- the white sphinx
- flowers
- the dying sun